The Fairy First Day

By Mickie Matheis • Illustrated by Victoria Patterson
Based on the teleplay by Jonny Belt and Robert Scull

Random House 🏠 New York

rhcbooks.com

ISBN 978-1-9848-9258-4

Printed in the United States of America

10 9 8 7 6 5 4 3 2 1

Butterbean flew through the town of Puddlebrook as fast as her fairy wings could carry her. Her two best friends, Poppy and Dazzle, and her little sister, Cricket, tried hard to keep up.

"Butterbean, slow down!" Cricket called.

"What are you so excited about?" asked Dazzle.

"You'll see," Butterbean promised.

"*Ta-da!* Here we are!" Butterbean announced. "This is our new café."

The fairies looked at the boarded-up building before them.

"It doesn't *look* very new," Poppy said skeptically.

"It will be when we fix it up," Butterbean replied. "Besides, I can't help feeling that there's something about this place—something magical!"

"I've always wanted to open a café with my best fairy friends. Poppy's a whiz at cooking, so she'll run the kitchen. Dazzle loves to keep things organized, so she'll take care of the front counter and make her *fairy* yummy smoothies. And Cricket loves helping—so she'll help all of us. We'll serve breakfast, lunch, dinner, desserts—everything! I can't wait to get started!"

Butterbean had wonderful plans for the café.

"With a pinch of patience and a helping of hard work, I know we can make this the *fairy* best café in all of Puddlebrook!" she declared to her friends.

"Let's get cooking!" they cheered as they fluttered inside.

Meanwhile, across the brook . . .

. . . there was another café—Marmalady's Café! It was run by Ms. Marmalady and her two assistants, Spork and Spatch.

Ms. Marmalady served only one thing—marma-loaf! It was green, gloppy, smelly, and not very appetizing.

"Nobody comes to eat my delicious marma-loaf," Ms. Marmalady said.

"That's because it doesn't taste very good," Spatch replied.

"Well, too bad, because this is the only café in town," Ms. Marmalady sneered. "And I intend to keep it that way."

Ms. Marmalady didn't know that the fairy friends were getting Butterbean's Café ready for its grand opening. . . .

In the old building, Cricket had discovered a mysterious box. She showed it to her sister. Butterbean noticed FOR THE FAIRY FINISH written on it. When she read the words aloud, sparkles suddenly began to dance around the box. The top opened and a magical whisk floated out!

Butterbean waved the whisk, and a trail of sparkles made the girls' wings look like yummy sugar cookies! The whisk also enchanted Poppy's spoon, gave Dazzle a magical stylus, and made something special for Cricket.

"What is this?" Cricket asked.

"That's an icing bag," Poppy said. "You can decorate cakes with it!"

The girls used their new magical tools to put the finishing touches on the café. Everything looked perfectly *perfect*!

Just then, the front door opened and a boy on a skateboard zipped in. "Delivery for Dazzle!" he called.

Dazzle was excited to see what he had brought.

"My name's Jasper," said the boy. "Wow, you really fixed up this old place."

Butterbean thanked him and explained that it was the café's opening day. She told him that most of their ingredients would be ordered fresh from nearby farms, and she could use a speedy delivery person like him.

Butterbean offered Jasper a job at the café. She even gave him really fast wings with her magical whisk. He fluttered around the café and high-fived Butterbean.

"I'm the newest member of the Bean Team!" he said proudly. Then he and Cricket flew off to deliver the invitations for the café's grand opening.

At her own café, Ms. Marmalady was spying on her new neighbors. "Do they think they can just flutter into town and open a brand-new café?" she muttered.

She didn't want anyone to go to Butterbean's grand opening, so she ordered Spork and Spatch to steal all the invitations Cricket and Jasper delivered. And they did just that.

Meanwhile, Butterbean was busy baking wing-shaped cookies for the grand opening when she noticed some writing on her whisk. It was a spell! She read it aloud: *"With a flick of this whisk and a flutter of wing, these magical beans will do their thing.'"*

Suddenly, colorful beans magically filled the box. There was a Sparkle Bean, a Swirly Bean, and even a Flutter Bean.

A magical whisk and magical beans? Butterbean was thrilled! There really *was* something special about her café, and she couldn't wait to share it with the rest of Puddlebrook!

Soon the girls were ready to open the café. They were excited to greet their customers!

But when they looked out the front door, no one was there.

Butterbean was determined to have the grand opening they'd worked so hard for. "There's got to be something we can do," she said.

That was when she remembered the magical beans. She chose a special one, then waved her whisk over it and said the spell: *"With a flick of this whisk and a flutter of wing, this Flutter Bean will do its thing."*

The wing-shaped cookies flew off the counter and fluttered through Puddlebrook, leading a crowd of townspeople to the café.

Even Spork and Spatch were unable to resist the magic.
"Oh, freezer burn," Ms. Marmalady grumbled. She knew
Butterbean's Café was going to be a huge success.

Butterbean's Café was officially open for business!

"Running a café is going to be a lot of work. But doing it with my little sister and my best friends is the *fairy* best thing I could wish for. Everything's better when we make it together!"